STOMP, STOMP!
A DINO ROMP

By Bob Kolar

North
South

FOR LISA

Copyright © 1997 by Bob Kolar
First published in the United States, Great Britain, Canada,
Australia, and New Zealand in 1997 by NorthSouth Books, Inc.,
an imprint of NordSüd Verlag AG, CH-8005 Zürich, Switzerland.

This edition first published in the United States, Great Britain, Canada,
Australia, and New Zealand in 2014 by NorthSouth Books, Inc.,
an imprint of NordSüd Verlag AG, CH-8005 Zürich, Switzerland.

Distributed in the United States by NorthSouth Books Inc., New York 10016.

Library of Congress Cataloging-in-Publication Data is available.
A CIP catalog record for this book is available from The British Library.
The artwork was created with watercolor dyes on Winsor & Newton paper.
ISBN: 978-0-7358-4169-7
Printed in China by Leo Paper Products Ltd.,
Kowloon Bay, Hong Kong, January 2014.

1 3 5 7 9 · 10 8 6 4 2

www.northsouth.com

Hee-hee.

THUMP.

WHUMP!

STOMP,
STOMP!

PLOP!

STOMP, STOMP!

BOOM, POW!

POUNCE.

TROUNCE!

Gotcha now!

STOMP,

STOMP,

STOMPITY?

STO

MP!

Bye-bye.